MW01230990

OBSCURA AND WORLDS BEYOND

A COLLECTION OF STRANGE TALES

TRAVIS GVBERVD WYRMWOOD

NIGHT COOK
Obscura File no. 0209

7:30 PM

The sun set on Ichor, Wisconsin in the rearview while Barry Valentine's voice chimed through the radio. *"Hello, hello, my night owl friends. Whether you're getting off work to catch your final groove of the day, or you're in it with me for the long haul—"*

Behind the wheel, Garfield Anderson said "I'm in it, all right. You know I'm in it."

"—Starts off with a classic," continued the radio host, running the track.

"All right," said Garfield. "Another night, another dollar."

The lyrics to Chicago's 25 or 6 to 4 kicked in, and he turned it up so he couldn't hear himself talk. Garfield sang along with Peter Cetera until he pulled his fixer-upper Ford flatbed into the parking lot.

Garfield rolled the windows up and the engine died, the last riffs of the song cutting early. "Another night, another dollar."

Parking in the back was a pain, the doors locked past seven PM, and the motion sensor light never seemed to kick on when he needed to find the right key. Also, though he'd never admit it, Garfield was afraid of the dumpsters out back in that weird hermit shack built to keep refuse out of the weather. The motion light clicked on and he went inside.

"They're on the way," said a nurse to two more scrubs-wearing thirty-somethings. "She's stable, just bring her out. It's easier if she's close to the doors."

Garfield typed six digits into a punch clock with his knuckle and walked through the doors to his kitchen. The afternoon cook had the kitchen borderline clean, for his thick head. Garfield knew most of that night would be spent cleaning the equipment, few food orders came in past midnight, except for the occasional dementia patient. Mostly, he fed the night staff and kept the lights on so the owner of the nursing home could call it a 'full service' establishment.

"What do you have for me, Mister Valentine?" He turned on the smudgy radio under the food preparation table, set as always to FM 99.9. The Stones' *Wild Horses* played in the florescent-lit kitchen as the first round of nursing staff came through. The morning cook had decided on mashed potatoes and meatloaf for tonight, and since it was already made, Garfield went along. "First thing I'd change is the food," he murmured to himself, opening the oven.

"What was that?" asked the seafoam green scrubs across the serving line, a nurse named Michael.

"Nothing, Mike. How are the residents tonight?"

"You know how they get when it's a full moon. I swear they aren't awake long enough to see the damn thing, but they still get going like animals. Mavis Vailer took a pretty good fall, but she'll be fine after a night in a real hospital."

"Don't sell yourself short, my friend, this place has all the charms of a bleached-out hospital. What can I get for you tonight? Bright eyes cooked us up some loaf, or I can whip up a sammy."

9 PM

The freezer behind the prep line hummed with a fury, and Garfield Anderson had spent the last forty-five minutes moving boxes of food to unblock the sputtering machine trapped within. Garfield liked the freezer. No lock meant no anxiety of being turned into a popsicle, and the night staff rarely went looking around in the kitchen. If he wanted to escape, that was it: his hideaway, his icy lair.

"Am I the only one who puts these things away?" He lifted a box and decided it was okay, something to do to pass the time. "Of course," he muttered as a bag fell through the bottom of a box he lifted, throwing its contents to the freezer-burnt floor. He looked under the shelving and saw his mess, then went to grab a broom.

"Gary, how's it goin?" said a B unit nurse walking through the kitchen.

Garfield said, "Another night, another dollar as they say."

"Does anyone say that but you? What's on tonight, Gar? I saw Mike chowing down on some meatloaf, I'll take a hot meal over a cold one any night."

"Yea, well, the weather sure is changing, isn't it? Here," he handed a to-go box full of warm food over the counter, "this should keep your hands warm while you walk back. I hope someone left the lights on for you, those crazies would make it awful hard to take it easy."

"The B unit is fucking scary at night, Gar, real fucking scary on nights like this. You saw Dolores in your cafeteria last week, right? She got transferred to my building after what happened. It's just a bunch of loose nuts and bolts over there without a toolbox to put them in."

Garfield said, "Yea, I hear ya, that was wild what happened, I couldn't work it on your side. It's bad enough what I hear from the nurses over here sometimes. These oldies are like glass and paper, and their minds are no different. Like Dolores, I think her mind just fell apart."

"Jesus, Gary, I have to go back there. It's not that bad, they're still people. We'll be old and senile like them someday too."

"You're right about that, abso-fucking-lutely right. Anyway, enjoy that hot food. I have a situation in the freezer."

The B unit nurse gave Garfield the thankful nod, which sealed their workplace acquaintanceship. Back in the freezer, Garfield swept what he could, moved the rest of the boxes, then swept the rest.

"This is ugly, real ugly." A mess of icy foodstuff a decade old tumbled out as he swept the furthest corners. "Christ, guys, we should hire a goddamn professional."

"What is that?" The pile of forgotten food was a freezer-burned mess, but there was something else too. Garfield kicked at a seamless metallic object the size of a cellphone half covered by year-old tator tots. "What the hell is that?"

"Hey!" Banging on the freezer door. "Hey!" someone called out again, louder this time. Even in the muffling freezer, it was a yell. Garfield saw through the small square of glass in the door that his *favorite* nurse was ready to eat.

He left his frozen lair. "Are you trying to give me a heart attack, Jan?"

Jan said, "Are you trying to starve me out, Garfield?"

5

"Meatloaf or sandwich?"

"Bologna sandwich, extra mayo, extra mustard. I have three residents all hungry for a hot meal, set those up for me too."

Garfield made the food without a word. "Anything else tonight, Janet?"

A black box on her hip buzzed, and she said she'd be back in a minute.

Garfield said, "I guess the residents will be getting a cold meal after all." Jan slipped around a corner while the food he packed up sat on his counter. "Oh, well." He turned around to reenter the freezer. *What the hell was that thing?* He saw the lights had been turned out inside his lair.

"Did I turn that off?" He went inside and pulled the string in the center of the frozen room, careful to avoid the pile he'd swept while stepping through the darkness. The light turned on with a satisfying click and lit the room with a yellowy glow.

"Hey, where'd you go?" He grabbed the broom propped against the shelving and spread the pile apart. *Where the hell did it go? God damn Janet.*

He finished up in the freezer and left his lair, being sure to leave the light on.

10:45 PM

Garfield Anderson took a break, without clocking out, of course, to sit in his car and write. From eleven to midnight, he fancied himself an author and wrote by the dome light in his truck. Tonight, he had no use for the dome light; the big moon lit his notebooks. The food Janet ordered still sat on the table as he finished preparing morning food for bright eyes. Garfield had taken one look at it and went to do his writing early. "Wasteful."

Thirty minutes in and he thought he'd written some fine work. It needed editing, but that's what his days off were for.

Just as he began writing the vampire's big entrance scene, he heard "Gary! Hey Garfield!" Mike pounded on the window, and he put his notebooks away.

Mike asked, "What are you doing out here?"

Garfield replied, "I'm taking a little break, Janet was getting to me."

"Dude, forget Janet. Take this." Mike tried handing Garfield a joint that both of their older brothers would've given two thumbs up.

"I'm off the stuff for a while," said Garfield. "The moon is enough tonight. This moon gets everyone crazy. I think I even write a little crazier."

7

"Well, come on out and watch my back by the dumpsters, finish your stories later."

"Yeah yeah, I'm on it, I could use a break anyway, my hand is cramping." Garfield exited his truck and proceeded to the hut housing the trash.

"Can't you smoke it out here?" Garfield asked, "It smells like old food and diapers in there."

"If one of the night nurses catches me, I'll lose my job, remember last time? You're the only one that's cool about it around here."

"Let's just hurry this up."

"Ditto, I agree on the smells. I'll be double-quick." Mike coughed and Garfield sat on the curb while the motion light turned off. Mike was taking his time, more than enough time for him to do his business.

After three minutes of waiting, Garfield called out, "Mike, what's up, man? You hiding in there somewhere?" He waited for a response but there was none. "Hey, Mike! God, where are you. All right, I'm going inside, I'm not playing games tonight. The scrubs are probably waiting on dinner too. I bet Janet needs her meals remade."

Garfield waited in silence again, hoping for a *"Fuck Janet, man!"* from the dumpsters. Nothing, Mike was probably waiting in the dark, just out of sight as you opened the gate to the dumpster's hut. He was waiting, Garfield was sure. "Enough, Mike. Good luck riding that high, seems like quite a trip. Just don't fall asleep out here."

Garfield stepped toward the door and the lights clicked on. He went for his keys and realized he already had them out, pushed between his fingers like Wolverine's knuckle blades. He let himself inside and stuck a brick in the doorway so Mike wouldn't have to unlock the door in the dark, the motion light would shut off soon and wait a full minute before sensing again. He'd be back soon.

11:30 PM

Janet's food still sat on the table, and the gravy ladled over the three resident's entrées had eaten through the bottom of the cheap clamshell to-go boxes the night shifters used when no dishwasher was on duty. *Fuck Janet, man.* "Mr. Valentine, what do you think?" He clicked on the ugly radio and FM 99.9 lived again.

"*And stay tuned folks,*" chimed Barry Valentine, "*we'll be taking a few calls from those who claim to have seen them, all that and more after this certified classic.*" Boston's *Peace of Mind* started up and Garfield was all in as he took care of the mess left on his counter. While the song played, he wondered where the hell Mike had gotten off to. "Someone's gonna find you, Mikey!" Garfield yelled to the empty room. The lights in the unused areas of the kitchen like the office and the dish pit were off, controlled by a timer. The song faded and the radio host took his time getting back on the air.

Garfield stood in the rattling white noise of his dimly lit kitchen, one door of separation between him and the rest of the nursing home. "Where is everybody?" he checked the time, 11:35 pm.

The radio chattered on and Garfield jumped a little.

"Goddamn it, Mister Valentine, you're gonna give me a heart attack."

"—*have a caller on the line and we are live. Now, caller, can you describe what you saw earlier tonight? Hello? Caller?*"

"*Black sun. Black sun. A flash and then, and then, I saw it. Black sun, the disks.*"

"*Uh, what was that? Can you try to describe for our listeners a little about what you saw tonight?*"

"*The light, burning light! The disks are here!*"

"*Sorry, folks, we must have taken a prank call, let's get right back into the music.*" A song began after a transition of switchboard garble that seemed to prove the caller had thrown the station off. Whatever song was playing, Garfield didn't really hear it, he was looking down.

"What the... you again?" The metallic thing he'd swept out of the deep freeze was between his feet.

"How did you make it out here, where'd you go before?" he picked it up, examining it in his palm. It was an unknown to him, probably a piece to one of the hundreds of machines kept in house to keep the residents alive. Probably.

"Did I turn the freezer light off? No. I left it on. I know I did. I must've gotten some second hand on that joint, where is my head at tonight?" He stood in front of the freezer door. The light was off, and the small window was a pane framing darkness. "I guess I don't need to be in there anyway. Better for the thing to stay off, maybe the timer is set up in there now too." He didn't think it was, but could give himself no better explanation. He stuck the metallic piece of medical equipment into his pocket and went to the cooler to throw another pan of bright eye's meatloaf in the oven. The second round of scrubs would be down to eat by midnight-thirty, and some would show up earlier. *Like Janet. Fuck Janet, man.*

1 AM

"Where is Mikey? Where is Janet? Where is everyone? Was there a meeting or a trip?" they'd never had a field trip past four PM, but that moon tonight was a sure spectacle, and the dreamy piece of his mind allowed it to be the answer. They were out stargazing. The whole place was out stargazing. He decided that if not out on a trip, everyone was asleep or maybe at the B unit next door. They could all be asleep, there were enough of those musty cots in unused rooms for the entire staff

"Oh well, more time to myself then. And Mister Valentine, of course." He poked at the dirty radio beneath his prep table and Valentine's voice filled the room. *How does this thing keep shutting off?* "What do you have for me, Barry?" Garfield asked to the empty room. The record Mister Valentine spun was a sultry groove, some nameless musician lost in recordings yet to be converted to a current format. Barry Valentine had a thousand songs from the swinging twenties, each more obscure than the last. He played them from one AM to three AM every weekday, a period Mister Valentine dubbed *Twilight Time*.

"I think I'll take a walk," Garfield said to himself as he finished dicing vegetables for a soup. "A walk to clear my head, I'm feeling fuzzy. And maybe I'll find Mike on the way." He washed his hands and walked to the doors Janet disappeared behind hours earlier. The doors that separated him from the rest, the doors that held back the chaos of a business where death is a daily visitor. "Mike better be right down this hall."

He wasn't, not in the hallway immediately before him anyway. "Let's see here..." Garfield ran his pointer finger over a full-color print in a loose plastic cover tacked to the wall. Nurses' names were listed in different colors by floor, building, and shift. His finger stopped at Mike's name. *Michael O'kelen- night shift- First Floor.*

"Mike?" Garfield called down the hall, hoping the residents wouldn't wake. No response, not from Michael or the other nurse assigned to *night shift- First Floor.* Garfield walked down the hallway under fluorescent lights, every fourth was dimmed while the others were off. "Hello?" He walked slowly, trying to peek through the cracks of a few resident's doors not fully closed. Most doors were closed, with new pictures of their children's families and old portraits of young men in armed-service uniforms on the walls between each—collections of ten or eleven pictures reflecting an entire lifetime. It made Garfield shiver. *They're still people.*

Abso-fucking-lutely. But not today. Not tonight. The door ahead, room 139, was ajar, propped far enough that he found staring into the room easy. It was mostly a graying black haze, except the large window and its ugly yellow blinds that almost glowed by the light of the moon behind them.

A silhouette appeared in front of the window with a sudden, jerking motion. Then it was motionless, not moving an inch after the initial frantic appearance. "What the?" Garfield's heart pounded in his ear, "Hello? Do you need assistance? Let me find a nurse." Garfield was petrified, standing in the long moony shadow cast by that silhouette. The fuzziness returned, emanating from his pocket and scrambling his brain like television static. The silhouette twitched violently, contorting and scuttling closer.

Garfield said, "Do you need help? What can I do to help you?" It came closer and Garfield asked a third time. "There's a nurse somewhere around here, do you need some help? I'll go find them for you."

Garfield was gone in a flash, back down the hall, through the doors and into his kitchen. Safe. His eyes went straight to the cutting board on his prep table, and the freshly sharpened eight-inch blade resting on it. It was a thing right at home in the kitchen but also comfortable in Mrs. Voorhees' slashing hands. She was a cook too, the camp cook, Garfield thought.

He laughed into his empty kitchen and said, "Welcome to camp crystal lake! That resident must think I'm a loon, running off like that. They probably needed real help, there are a hundred things a nursing home patient might need. It's this moon, messing with my head. Messing with the residents too, that's it. It's the moon that's getting to me, and everyone else is sleeping. Well, everyone besides 139 and Barry Valentine." Garfield turned the radio back on, no longer questioning why it might be off. It was an off sort of night.

The next hour went by in a fuzz of twenties swing. Mister Valentine's Twilight Time spun on without ads, and Garfield found it extremely easy to slip into autopilot. His headspace was filled with no-name songs and the static that came built-in to that era. One minute, he was tossing his diced vegetables into a pot. The next, he was stirring a completed soup. In the swinging section of Mister Valentine's twilight time, hours slipped away.

3:35 AM

Garfield opened his eyes from what he called an 'occupancy hazard' working the night shift. "You're damn liable to fall asleep, running the shift on your own. I can't be hassled if it happens," he would say when anyone caught him. No one had walked into his kitchen tonight to find him half asleep, head down on the counter. No one had come in for a long time. It was the ringing in the room, like a dog whistle siren he was barely hearing. It was accompanied by a crystalline headache, one that held itself together until he focused on it, then crashed like a chandelier to the floor.

"Ah god my head, what's that noise coming from?" He rubbed his eyes and looked around his kitchen, still empty, not even Mister Valentine. "What is with tonight?" He bent, clicked the radio on, but nothing came from it. He looked for the cord connected in the back. "It's plugged in alright, so what the hell?" He stood and his head pounded in dismay.

Upon standing, Mike, Janet, and the B unit nurse were in his kitchen.

Garfield said, "What the hell, guys, where have you been? Was there a star gazing party or something? Way to leave me out."

Mike said, "Come with us, Gary. There's something you have to see."

Janet added, "Come on Gar, let's go."

"Gar?" Garfield asked. "Since when do you call me anything but my full name?"

"It's an emergency," replied Janet.

"She's right, Gary," said the B unit nurse.

All three stepped forward, the B unit nurses beer gut pressed tight in teal scrubs against the counter. "What are you talking about?" Garfield asked, backing until he felt an icy slab at his back. He turned for a moment, startled, and saw his reflection in the dim square of glass on the door to the freezer. He couldn't look away, as he saw the three figures in the reflection coming toward him. Mike was grabbing for the knife on the table.

Garfield turned and said, "Dude, what are you doing?" then made a break for it around the counter as they were climbing over it. He ran around the corner and through the double doors, into the hallway of the nursing home.

All the lights were out. Every door was wide open as far as he could tell, with moonlight pouring into the hallway from each one. He ran, briefly looking into them. He saw contorted silhouettes standing motionless in the glowing yellow as he passed each room.

At the end of the hall, passing 139 on his left and 140 on his right, there was another turn. More resident rooms were down that hall, and an empty nurses' station at the far end.

"Come on, Gar!" Mike yelled from somewhere behind.

"We really need you, Gary!" yelled Janet. "We need everyone!"

Garfield pushed into a closed door down the middle of the hallway. Most were closed past the corner he took. He shut the door behind him and whispered, "Is anyone here? Any residents? I think we're in danger, the staff has gone crazy." He waited for a response as he crouched and crawled, trying to find cover quickly. He whispered again, "Hello, is anyone here? Do you have a phone in this room? We need to call for help."

The bed was empty, and the room wasn't much more than that. Nothing under the bed, and no feet behind the curtains like in the movies. "A phone, thank Christ almighty." He put it to his ear and dialed.

"The number you are dialing is no longer in service."

"What?" Garfield put the phone down and picked it up again, then redialed 911.

"The number you are dialing is no longer in—" He tried again, and again. Nothing. He slammed the phone down with a loud clang and immediately regretted it.

He huddled in the corner on the far side of the bed near the window. The window! Garfield pulled the blinds back, ready to escape.

"How could I forget!" he drew in a breath to curse at the top of his lungs but clenched his fists white and held it back. The windows had an easy sliding glass frame, but behind it was a crisscrossing cage like a prison cell. Sometimes, the patients liked to escape. The families, never thrilled to hear their loved one was run down by a car past midnight, insisted on extra security.

Garfield went back to the corner and listened to the three nurses trudge up and down the hallway, probably deciding where the noise came from. "Of course, they know where it came from," he said to himself, "I'm trapped. I'm fucking trapped."

?:?? AM

The three nurses stood outside room 166. They stood there, as Garfield could only guess, to scare the shit out of him. They had him, and if this is what they wanted to do with their night, they were doing it well. "I gotta get out of here, I gotta get out of here," he whispered repeatedly, until it was an incoherent jumble.

A knock on his door, pleasant and shy like room service at an upscale hotel. It shot fear through his system to match the dog whistle headache coming back with a vengeance. The fuzzy static of a CRT television filled his mind. Wind rushed through the open window, kicking the blinds up, making Garfield jump.

The knocking started again and did not stop. Louder, it rose to a terrible pounding. The pounding matched his heartbeat, and from the opposite side of the bed, a wood panel slid open.

"Oh my god the fucking closet!" cried Garfield, gripping the sides of the window frame. All three nurses must have been pounding at the door. It was a blinding rattle of sound.

A hand emerged from between linens in the closet of the dark room, the fingers were long, much longer than any human's. The door to the room swung open and the nurses piled in as another hand raised from the closet. The skinny arms bent with too many joints, grabbing at the panel of the door and the side wall to propel the rest of its unseen body forward. The nurses came forward single file.

Mike said, "We need you, Gary."

"Get away from me with that knife, Mikey!"

Behind Mike, Janet said, "It's time, Garfield. We need everyone."

Garfield yelled, "Fuck you, Janet!" and secured his grip on the sides of the window frame. He swung his body forward feet first and kicked as hard as he could through the crisscross bars.

He was free. He stood up on the far side of the back lot and saw his truck at the far end, near the garbage shack. The motion light clicked on. He was in pain from falling out the window onto pavement but felt lighter somehow and moved as fast as he could.

No one followed him, and for a second, he decided he had imagined the entire thing, that he'd gone loony working the night shift on a full moon. Then, he saw something as he looked back. A metallic object on the pavement near the broken window cage. The unknown that he'd stuffed in his pocket.

"I forgot about you," he said to himself as he neared his truck, "But I don't want to know a thing about tonight. I'm getting out of here and never coming back."

Garfield checked his front pockets, then his back, and felt on the sides as if he had khakis on. "Where are my keys, where are my keys." He trembled, realizing they were still inside. "I'll hoof it then, whatever it takes to get out of here, I'm going home."

His truck revved on as he stood outside it. The windows rolled down and the radio kicked on, FM 99.9 as always. The intro to Supertramp's *Take the Long Way Home* began playing, turning up to ten and past it.

Garfield was basked in intense moonlight, the cloud cover passed. Except, as he looked up, he saw there was no cloud cover. There were no clouds, and no moon either. The twilit sky was filled with black disks. A disk above blocked the moon but pointed its own celestial searchlight on Garfield. He vanished from the parking lot as the radio played on.

Take the long way home.
Take the long way home.

JUBAL AND THE ORACLE OF TIME

Few tales from the drifting island of Song still exist. Records of the island's authenticity cannot be corroborated. Little is known beyond that if it did exist, it must have existed in many different places throughout our history. These are the recovered journal entries of a young, controversial scholar named Jubal.

– Donated for private use by the Cor Laven Ark

DAY 1 AT THE TEMPLE OF SONG

The wind had guided me at steady pace to the temple seated atop the island called Song. The curving, red and black architecture set the place apart from the hills behind it. A pond spun with lily pads and lotus flowers to my right, while charms hung from pink, budding trees to my left.

I had passed through a gate and turned to look down onto the village so far below, and the sprawling forests all around. The ocean was almost out of sight, covered by a low and steady fog. Waves I could barely see were curling around the island. The water flowed as if my island home shifted in the sea, carving a path on the ocean floor.

The air was filled with new spring dew and still held the nip of coldness I could see in the snow that topped the peak of the mountain the temple rested on. The peak was not so far away as it had been a day ago, when I started the climb with only my calligraphy supplies to carry. Even since then I think I have grown some, leaving my family behind for this obstinate calling of mine. Stairs led to that peak behind the temple. They were cut into the mountain itself, I noticed. Flags dotted the path up, a tattered, sun-stained red.

Sat on a bench under the trees I saw my companion

Recorder, the only other student on the mountain. His name was Cainos. Cainos climbed to the temple weeks prior, and had already built a distaste for the master we would learn under. Even then though, as I walked between the trees and the pond, I could see his anger at my arrival. He probably thought I would disrupt his education.

"Hello," I bowed, and he nodded, not bothering to stand and return my gesture. I passed by the bench Cainos sat on and came to a tall, red door. It was cracked inward an inch, and as I knocked with the golden knocker, it pushed in and I saw the temple's main hall for the first time. It was sprawling with pillars of beautiful wood extending up and out, supporting many levels of tilted roofs above. The floor was of pure white marble or ivory or pearl, a single mass that spanned the whole palace. In the center, a golden bell hung three stories in the air.

Under the enormous bell sat three cushions. The first time I stared at those used-looking, burgundy cushions on the solid pale floor I knew I would spend countless days knelt on them. Cainos must have known as well and was tired of it. He had come for knowledge in a ravenous sort of way, far beyond the goals of someone who might simply hand lessons down from one generation to the next.

A ray of sun peaked through the building from precise angles, shining the light to the back of the temple. That is where I first saw my master, the Sage Recorder I knew as Zhou.

DAY 2 AT THE TEMPLE OF SONG

I slept with some disturbance during my first night at the Temple of Song. It seems that a small animal kept me up all night, gnawing or scratching at the outside of the palace. To my sleepless mind, it became horrible, like the scraping claws of a beast out to haunt me. I know such ideas are foolish, and I set them aside as I began my day. I will check in after breakfast and prayer. I think my first day as a student shall be filled with much learning indeed.

DAY 2, AFTER BREAKFAST

I thought, though I know not to say anything to a man who's already turned to me with distaste, that I saw something peculiar about Cainos while we ate. He kept his robe sleeves uncuffed, covering his arms. I hadn't seen this style in any village on my way up the mountain, but I did not question it. His stare is piercing and I care not for it. I have not heard a single word yet from Master Zhou, who simply sat and drank tea and watched the lily pads spin at breakfast.

At prayer he was absent completely, but Cainos led it with some degree of spite. I thanked him, for I was still new to the customs of the temple and he had learned them in the weeks previous, but he said not a word. I haven't seen him since he left Zhou and myself at the pond while he went inside. I wonder what he does when we are not around? I wonder when Zhou will speak up, but I will not be so nubile as to force his tongue. I think all this quiet observation might be the first step in his lessons. We will see.

DAY 3 AT THE TEMPLE OF SONG

I haven't slept since arrival, except for short disturbing intervals of napping by the pond. I always wake to that cruel scratching; that scraping will not leave my head. I think if it does not stop soon, I will have to ask Zhou about it. He still has not spoken, but led us in a silent prayer.

Note: when I say prayer, I mean something more akin to a dance or ritualistic movement. It is hard to explain by mere text, but those movements become our prayer to the goddess of time and her children.

I noticed, while we prayed, that Cainos's sleeves would bunch at his elbows. His movements were too quick to see with any amount of detail, but I saw markings of some kind on his forearms. They looked fresh and some were deep and still releasing blood. Zhou took notice and glared at Cainos, but the prayer continued. I wonder at the strangeness of this place. I came here to record the histories of our people, yet I have not seen a single calligraphy set but my own which I use in private since arriving.

Aside from Prayer, Zhou has still only had tea in my presence.

DAY 5 AT THE TEMPLE OF SONG

I could not write yesterday. There was absolutely no time. I was right about the silent analyzation being our first test here. Today Zhou handed out parchment and we wrote out all that we had noticed at this temple so far, in the most exact and intricate chronology you might imagine.

My notes differed only slightly from what is written in this diary so far, as I did not want to offend my fellow student or Master Zhou. Combined with their entries on our time so far, we had a minute by minute analysis from three sides. When we were done, Zhou said that that was our prayer, and swept all our writing away. He said to repeat the exercise again, and that tomorrow we would do the same.

I think he means to do this every day to us, while adding the current day to our analysis. Is this the great Sage Recorder Zhou that I have heard so much about? Is this all the recording I might be doing? His title seemed to promise more, but I will not speak up. Neither of them have yet. I will write more tomorrow, if there is time. For the first time I do not hear that terrible scratching, and will sleep well, I think.

DAY 12 AT THE TEMPLE OF SONG

Two days ago Master Zhou finally spoke at length to us. We have been at our daily recording habit for almost a week now, but Zhou said our history was incomplete. He threw out all of our writings to date, saying that we would have to start again. This time, however, we would start on the week previous to our first recorded day.

He stressed the importance or remembering each detail of each day, no matter how long it may take to remember. The result has been a constant need to examine and reexamine the past, to make it perfect so he might leave my writings be, instead of discarding them.

Master said that nothing would come of imperfect histories, but caught his words near the end and I think meant not to say them. The words brought an awful glow to Cainos's eyes and I know he was seething with hate. Cainos, more than I, seems to be here to do more than record the trivialities of his silent life. I write this by light of a candle in my room, listening to the scratching again.

DAY 12, AFTER NIGHTFALL

I couldn't very well sleep with that despicable scratching. I made the decision, after holding off for so many days, to go and see what it was. I exited my chamber and walked across the cold, solid floor. All the candles of the temple were put out, though in the daytime there could be hundreds all burning in a single room. It was silent, and I still do not know where Zhou sleeps at night.

I had first checked near Cainos's room but heard nothing and figured him asleep. I slipped outside the tall red door of our near-silent palace. Outside, the breeze rustled a few wind chimes and for a second I thought that was the noise I came to find. When the winds died down, however, I heard a sound like snickering or mocking to oneself. It was a mad little laugh from around the back of the temple, and I braced myself to look.

I came upon Cainos. Though my lamp light gave away my coming, he did not run. He was lost in some time other than this. He was propped against the temple, a book in his lap and a knife in one hand. The temple wall was covered in in overlapping carvings of a single design.

Blood trickled down his arm from small, intricate blade strokes. The carving in his skin matched those on the wall, only fouler than I had seen before. I knew what it was. I saw the book his pale face tilted over and the page he copied it from. It was a language, some old language out of a book he'd stashed in the ferns behind the temple. I promptly shut the book and removed the blade from his hand, tossing it into the inclined woods behind us.

I am not a strong man, but I could easily lift him over my shoulder and carry him around to the front before setting him down. His weight was that of an infant, as if the stuff that filled him was temporarily elsewhere. I knew not what else to do, had never needed Zhou after dark, and so I ran inside and rang the golden bell.

Zhou appeared behind me, I'm not sure from where, and followed me as I ran out the door again. We brought Cainos inside, and Zhou grabbed the book his student had apparently stolen. This was the only the second time that Zhou said anything more than a few words to me, and I still reel in their meaning.

He told me, while Cainos lay unconscious before us, "Cainos has much to learn. You do as well. What we do here is the only thing in all of Roon that needs, without question, to continue. We are the Recorders. What histories we write will shape the future, for what has been written can be learned from. In the same vein, what we learn can become the future itself. There are ways of deducing, when all calculations are in order, the ways the universe might unfold. Through constant recording, we give ourselves pieces of that equation, which we must only string together to complete."

I said to him with complete disbelief, "What we write will determine the future?"

"And so much more," Zhou answered, "There are specific words and symbols that can help to lock a historical event in place, even one that has not yet happened. These are the greatest and most dangerous tools a Recorder can use."

I spoke out of turn, though Zhou did not seem to care, "And when are these tools bestowed upon us?"

Zhou said, "Time has little meaning to me. I can say, though, that Cainos was not at all ready."

I was confused, "He has used those symbols?"

"Look at the wall—look on his arm, there. Those carvings are the start of a mechanism which could lock in specific futures. Do you see his eyes? His pupils are gone. Cainos is lost somewhere outside this time, experiencing some uncertain history. He found these far too early in his training, with no knowledge on how to use them. He is in a place between time."

I nearly left at that examination, unable to accept the things Master Zhou was saying to me.

He saw my discomfort and continued, "These are all things to be learned in time; you've been flooded with too much information. Focus again on your writings, on your daily recordings. Go, Jubal, take rest while you can. I will handle this, and all shall be better in the morning."

At that, I felt extremely tired from weeks of unsatisfying sleep and went at once to my chamber for respite.

DAY 13 AT THE TEMPLE OF SONG

As detailed in my previous entry, I was extremely tired last night, and only left my chamber when the sun of late morning joined my bed to wake me. I came to my cushion in the main hall, both Zhou and Cainos were knelt in reflection and I joined them without a word.

A bird in the pond outside sang out and the sound resonated in the bell above us. Zhou stood after the bell's resounding was complete and spoke.

"Today, our lessons advance onward. You have been recording the events of the day and all days prior. This is good practice for recorders, but it is obviously not enough to satisfy my students." He looked, in a frame of silence, at Cainos, then me. "I understand, the possibilities of a recorder seem unbound from the view of the common people, but common people you are no longer. This is not a job of traveling to times far beyond your own to see what the world may be like. By doing so, you almost absolutely ensure that that future will not happen. Cainos, truly you have failed so far. Whatever you might have seen last night in your time lost stupor, it can now never be so. You effectively change the future, with little insurance on what takes its place."

Cainos looked down during this, not his usual silent yet tenacious self.

Zhou continued, "Today, I teach you how you might fulfil a certain future. Just as you have written all of your days so far, I want you today to write what might happen tomorrow. Write it in as much detail as you catalogue the past. Do this for a week, every day adding a day to your future prediction."

I asked, baffled by what he said, "Will what we predict truly play out?"

"On the smallest of scales, yes, it might. To a visible degree, only maybe. The symbols of a Recorder are needed to hold a lasting change in history. Still, this will focus your minds on the futures and not the pasts."

He ended his lecture with a silent prayer and told us to begin the recordings at once. I was lost in all the things he said, half sure that I was doing nothing at the top of a mountain, half sure that every word I write from now on might come true.

I took up the future saying endeavor easily enough, mostly adding in things from my previous days, imagining the way they take shape. Soon though, I seemed to have new ideas of what might come, and I struggled to push them out of my mind.

DAY 21 AT THE TEMPLE OF SONG

I have, over this last week, been feverishly writing things that happen in the future, and willing them to be with all my strength, no matter how mundane. Last night, I heard the scraping sound for a short time, but it quieted fast so that I gave it not a thought.

This morning when I got to my cushion, all was not well. Zhou stood under the bell while a series of bird calls echoed through it. The birds were something of my own design—I had been writing that they would announce my coming to the temple hall every morning now since my identification of the future began. It is a funny thing to begin believing in things so outlandish as future sight, and even creation. I swim with these thoughts in my dreams, but do not bring them to light. I admit that just thinking of them might undo the fragile bond I'm forming with the 'Shards of Axidros', a place set apart from time that Zhou has referenced on several occasions.

As I was saying, all was not well upon my entrance, even with the chorus of birds singing which I myself seemed to summon. Cainos was nowhere to be seen, and Zhou seemed acutely aware of that. We stood in silence under the bell for several minutes before Zhou spoke.

"Cainos has done the unthinkable. He has written himself

into the far future and marked it with Recorder symbols. The fool is lost in time far outside his own. I have read his writings, his future-tellings. He has placed himself there in hopes of becoming the hero of that time. He's written a cataclysm that he himself can prevent. Gods, he has Doomed ages of Roon still yet to be."

I was made to feel something of a fool myself, having thought merely of birds and daily habits in the last week. While I wrote of the uninspired, he thought himself up as a legend. I felt I'd wasted my week.

I said to Zhou, "How could you let this happen? How did he know the symbols of a Recorder? What was he taught in his few weeks before me, that I was not?" I was ashamed, and still am, at my outburst toward Master Zhou. He looked immediately beaten.

Zhou explained, "I tried—I tried to stop him, to right his behavior. He has an excellent memory you know, and other skills that placed him here. Just as you have. He is more deviously clever than you though, he snuck into my personal library before you arrived. I caught him and was sure I found all he was stealing, but the book you found with him a week ago told otherwise. Still I continued teaching him, hoping he would see the error of his ways. I see now his ambition is driven by selfish desire. A savior, why did he think of being such a thing? With his mind like it is, the eons of waiting he will do between his own time and his recordings will drive him to become something else entirely"

I asked, "What is there that can be done?"

"Go on with a prayer of your own and write your predictions. Reach out another week with your thoughts, go further than before. That is all for me today, I will be in my private library. I hope to see your birds again tomorrow. I know you've been writing them in as your arrival chime. All is not lost yet, Jubal. Keep recording."

DAY 30 AT THE TEMPLE OF SONG

I haven't seen Zhou Song in a week. I've had a flock of different colored birds announce my arrival to the temple's main hall for six days now, but I'm the only one to see it. I have not felt this lonely in some time.

Even on my journey to this place, the people from each village knew me to some extent, or had at least heard of my travels. I was well learned among my farming village and set out to be a Recorder long ago. I was companioned by a pack animal by day and inn keepers at night. Now however, I felt alone.

The lily pads twirled in the pond, supporting a cluster of tadpole eggs on its submerged stem. I had started writing that bit a week ago too, and now a few were hatching to life. Did I create those, or simply guess at the possibility of their life using the algorithms of the past? These were the musings of my lonely mind.

I pray daily, and continue my record of the future, going out weeks further every day. Tomorrow, I'll have written and rewritten records of every day in the coming year. Next week, I might have over five years written on future events. I hope by then to have found Master Zhou.

DAY 60 AT THE TEMPLE OF SONG

I think I've been alone in this temple for over a month. At first, I thought miscellaneous noises in the surrounding land was the stirring of my master somewhere beneath the temple. Now, I think it is just the stirring of wind and trees.

Not a day passes where I do not record both past and future events. I've gone back in time as far as I can with my own memories, and now use a few books I have found in the main hall to supplement my record. As far as future events, however, I seem to be very far ahead of schedule. The further ahead I write, the further I feel I *can* write.

I have stopped listing the years in which I jump ahead, and instead refer to them in ages. With each passing day, the surety of what I record about both past and future is astoundingly accurate. I think I remember even writing about the books I found to continue my study of history. Did I place them there with my ink, or had they always been? I can't recall, but all of my records indicate they've been there.

DAY 65 AT THE TEMPLE OF SONG

The strangest thing happened to me while I recorded the far ages of Roon's future. I thought without question, that Cainos should be there. All the circumstances fit his presence, and the words nearly wrote themselves. He was a savior, a powerful ruler fighting a Titan of even older legend. He became a god among men in that duel, and the ink wouldn't stop flowing.

To my surprise, however, he did not stay a savior. My future rattled on, hundreds of years after his rise, and I saw that he was still there, still ruling in the old Titan's place. This future disturbed me, but I could not stop writing. I will finish with a prayer and watch the frogs jump near the pond. Such deliberate yet unconscious connections between me and my frogs is all I have for companionship.

DAY 66 AT THE TEMPLE OF SONG

I've come across Zhou in my records as I press further and further into the future. He seems to pop up everywhere for just a moment. My interpretation is that he has placed himself at those spots with the Recorder symbols as a way to prevent the tragedies of the future.

I wonder if he's already written everything I have? Is that what he was training me to do? I feel an odd connection to him through my records. The only way to understand further is to continue recording, a task that I alone now carry out.

DAY 100 AT THE TEMPLE
OF SONG

If it wasn't for the daily writing of my past and future, I would've forgotten there were once other people here. It is quiet, and even my frogs are quieting, ready to hibernate.

I see clearly, every day, the point where Cainos comes into my prediction. I see just as clearly the thousands of other points he tries to come in and alter things, only to be beaten by Zhou. Zhou appears and disappears from my records like clockwork, tiny blips along the way to let me know that that point in history is safe from Cainos's claim to power. Zhou was right: Cainos had gone mad in his time lost dreams of the future. He'd gone mad, and tried to make his madness a reality, only for Zhou to follow him into forever.

Zhou was there at every point but the last, when Cainos duels the old Titan and rises before a new people, far in the future. Why Zhou left it, I do not know. I can only think that after so many thousands of attempts, Cainos finally beat our master at his own game.

I felt defeated. My work as a Recorder somehow shined a light at the end of history, a time when one man brings all of humanity down with him. How could I let it happen?

Then, I began on another thought, one that hadn't yet

occurred to me. What if I write myself in, so I might stop Cainos from his eventual downfall? I looked through the books I'd studied and found new pages, but pages that looked familiar none the less. Intricate symbols lined the pages and there I was given the last tools I would need to stop Cainos.

DAY 101 AT THE TEMPLE
OF SONG

Today I set in recording all of what is to come, and all of what has been. I did this all before sunrise and watched a single frog jump from the lily pad that I so often admired, sending it twirling about the pond. I felt a sense of easiness in the morning sun as it touched me, and I looked on what I had written that day.

It was a history spanning all time, so far into the future my head spun as I read what the ink had formed on the page. The workings of the future are too vast to explain, and so I will not try. All I can say is that today, I completed it.

I wrote myself into every point in history that Cainos would attempt to infiltrate. I set myself one step ahead of him, watching his rise and fall in the split seconds between ages, countless times. I undid all of his works, placing myself there with the symbols I found in my books. There were countless battles over an infinity of times reaching into the gravest and brightest futures imaginable, but I stopped them all.

Then, I recorded something so appalling, and with such ease, that I began to tremble and tucked my record away. There, at the end of history, I stood, dominating everything. It made me sick to my stomach and I got up, unable to think anymore.

I gathered up my books and brought them to an area of the

palace I hadn't yet been, following a set of stairs to a near empty basement. There was a desk full of parchment and a calligraphy set similar to mine. Along the back there was an empty bookshelf that I quickly lined with the books I'd brought down.

It was then that I noticed how much time had passed. Months? Years? Decades? I stopped counting. The bushy white eyebrows in my peripherals answered for me. Was I always alone? Besides the descriptions in my records, I cannot remember anyone else ever living there.

I thought, if it is inevitable that I will rise at the end of all time, then I need to place symbols in my record that might stop it.

It was then that I first carved an intricate symbol, the Symbol of Cainos. I wrote of a devoted, tenacious scholar, traveling up to my temple. I wrote, too, of a younger scholar who would come a few weeks later. They would balance each other, I thought. I set my writings down at the sound of a voice calling for me in the halls above. It was a familiar voice.

"Master Zhou?" the voice called, "Master Zhou, It's me, your new apprentice, Cainos."

I went up the stairs and noticed how much younger he looked than I could recall. I supposed it was my own age that was truly surprising, but I quietly accepted the added years.

"Hello," I spoke, "I am Master Zhou Song. Are you my new Recorder?"

"I am." answered Cainos.

I said calmly and with all the time in the world, "Let us begin."

THE SUPER ELITE

Obscura File No. 0210

7:25 AM WEDNESDAY

Two friends drove down a country road watching the sun rise as 70's classics roared over the speakers. An excited female voice chimed through the radio of the flatbed Ford, *"Stay at the Super Elite, a retirement home unlike any other, right here in Ichor, Wisconsin."*

From the passenger seat, Bart turned the volume down and said, "I hate radio ads. They never get the sound mixing right, it's always turned up so much higher than the songs."

"They're harbingers of doom, Bart," said Nora, taking one hand off the steering wheel to raise a middle finger at the radio, "always bringing the songs to an end. And they're never about anything good, always fast-food ads and fancy shops we don't have."

Bart said, "Yea, where's all the 'freakshow coming to town' ads? That's what this place needs."

Nora said, "If that one ever comes on, you'll have to find yourself a new partner in crime, I'll be joining the caravan."

"Oh really? Well, Nora Grimwell, What's your carnival talent?"

"I'll be a fortune teller of course. Tarot cards and all that, you remember I used to give you readings all the time. I shoulda charged you for those."

Bart watched her drive and said, "Keep my tab open on that tarot business, Nor, I'm still waiting for those readings to come true. And Lucky for me I don't think the circus is coming anytime soon. When's the last time Ichor had a good shake up?"

Nora replied, "You mean something around here changing besides the two traffic lights or the seasons? Well, there was that old lady shouting about flying saucers on the radio a few years ago—"

"That barely counts, I'm still out here hearing about that so-called body farm hidden at a secret base out in the woods. We've trespassed on every mile of this county at one time or another and I haven't seen a thing."

Nora started laughing, "So we go from one crazy hick rumor to the next around here. What's new."

"I heard Bigfoot is moving to town soon."

They laughed as the budding farmland around them glistened with dew. The smell of manure wafted through the truck's open windows. They crinkled their noses and Nora put peddle to metal.

As they came to decidedly fresher air, Bart said, "You know, I've heard good things about that place."

"What place?"

"The old folks' home from the radio, the Super Elite. They pay better than the job we're headed now. And, we don't even have to deal with the darker side of nursing home employment, we can apply as cooks."

"Nora hit the blinker and pulled into the parking lot of a gray, two-story building. She looked at Bart and nodded, "Maybe after work I'll go online and fill out whatever forms they have. Another day stuck here, and I'll be fully convinced that I'm stuck in the twilight zone."

Bart held his hand on the door handle. "Maybe it's time for a career change."

4:30 PM FRIDAY

Nora sat in her truck after work waiting for Bart, daydreaming for a moment about never coming back. Her phone buzzed in her satchel, and she answered it before the Addams Family ring tone could snap more than twice. A bright female voice said, "Hello, is Nora Grimwell available?"

"This is her, who am I speaking with?"

"Oh good, I was hoping you would answer right away, I have wonderful news. This is Tressa with the Super Elite Extended Care Community and I've been excited to speak with you since I saw your application two days ago. You will of course have to come in for an interview to assure that you're the right fit, but we see no problems with your resume."

Nora moved the phone a few inches from her ear and looked out the window, smiting the gray two-story building with a glance. She grinned and brought the phone back, "That is wonderful news, I don't suppose I could come in for that interview tomorrow? I'm free all day."

There came a shuffle of papers, probably a calendar, then Tressa said, "Glad to hear it! I'll be here until 2 pm tomorrow, would you prefer before or after lunch?"

"After lunch would be best."

"1 pm it is then, I'll have someone waiting for you when you park, don't mind the guards. Do you need directions?"

"I'll find my way, thank you so much. And alright, I'll leave my throwing knives at home."

Laughter bubbled from the other end of the line before Nora could regret saying such a thing to the person who might be her new boss. Tressa ended the call with an upbeat "See you then!" and Nora closed her phone.

Bart pushed through the double doors of the shabby two-story building and took his hat off, raising both hands in the air while yelling, "I've escaped the Twilight Zone for another Weekend! Oh, Saturday how I've missed you!"

Nora thought he might fall to his knees in praise, but he continued toward the truck as she turned the key in the ignition. Bart opened the passenger door as the radio kicked on and they drove toward the sunset listening to Steely Dan's 'Do It Again', volume dialed all the way up.

12:50 PM SATURDAY

The parking lot of the Super Elite was enough to convince Nora she was doing the right thing. It was hard telling Bart she had an interview when he never got a call himself, but she suspected that was because of his driving record. Driving her old truck down a blue-lit corkscrew tunnel into the underground garage was like moving from rural America into a space station.

She slowed to a stop as the tunnel straightened and a gate blocked her path. A pane of glass on the left wall revealed the security room with two guards inside viewing various surveillance screens.

Nora cranked down her window and waved at them, "I'm here for an interview!"

Without a glance from either guard the gate made a single beep and raised. Nora pulled forward with a flourish of the engine and both guards jumped at the sound.

From there the tunnel opened onto the garage where, still doused in soft blue light, she drove slowly around the stadium sized lot dotted with support pillars.

She parked in the section marked *Guests and Employees* a few spaces from the other cars and sat in her truck, breathing steadily after rolling the window back up.

"It's just an interview," Nora whispered to herself, "Just an interview. No need to be nervous. Tressa basically said I have the job already. Don't mess this up. Don't go back to that Dingy office." With that push she stepped into the ambient blue light of the garage and locked her door.

The cars parked in the employee section were nearly all the same pearl white color, and though Nora counted a few different models, they were all a vision of the 1950s, with tail fins like a rocket ship and whitewall tires.

"What the Hell is an Absenio?" She read the same silvery name on the side of every vehicle.

A distinctly British male voice came from halfway across the lot, "Those would be our company cars. Now come along."

The man stood near a set of doors with the words 'The Super Elite' cut from stainless steel hanging above them.

"Hello? Are you speaking to me?"

"You are Nora Grimwell? The interview with Tressa is in three minutes, elevators are this way."

"Thank you, this place is already a bit overwhelming." She walked toward the man who turned and propped the door open.

He said, "Use any elevator on the left, the right side is for residents only. You understand."

"Sure, now what floor will take me to where I'm going?" Nora stepped into the lobby where six elevators lined the walls, three on either side. Fuzzy music from the early 20th century played and the scent of perfume that could only come with a large velvety squeeze pump brought her to another time.

The doorman said, "the thirteenth floor will bring you to Tressa's personal receptionist."

Nora pressed the summons button, calling any of the doors on the right to open. "Did you say thirteenth floor? From the outside I couldn't see much through the trees, is this building really so tall?"

She stepped inside the middle elevator before he replied and pressed '13', admiring the red carpeting and mirrored walls, and especially the small crystal chandelier which made the place feel like a ball room for one.

The doorman spoke from the lobby, "This building is not tall, Ms. Grimwell. It is *deep*."

The golden doors closed like the beak of a giant squid and Nora felt the elevator descend while an unremembered 1920 song fizzled on.

1:05 PM SATURDAY

Nora ran her hand through her hair and said, "Sorry I'm a minute late, when I was told this office was 13 floors underground, I had to press the buttons to a few other floors just to see if they were real. I've never heard of a place like this."

Tressa's receptionist stood behind a small desk off to the side of a yellow door with no apparent handle. "Yes of course," he said while twirling a pen, "It is rather odd when you think about it isn't it? I suppose I've gotten used to it. I'll notify her," he pointed toward the door with the pen, "and she will be with you as soon as possible."

Nora nodded and cleared her throat while brushing out as many wrinkles in her shirt as she could. A minute later, the yellow door pulled inward and a tall woman in an equally yellow suit emerged.

"Right this way," said Tressa with a toothy smile, motioning for Nora to come in, "This should be quick!"

Tressa went to sit behind her desk covered in nick-nacks and Nora took a seat opposite to her, trying hard to match the woman's smile as well as she could.

Nora let her shoulders relax and said, "You must be Tressa."

"What gave it away?" Tressa bubbled into laughter for a

moment before putting out her right hand, "So nice to finally meet you and put a face to the name. This is one of the Super Elite offices, though you won't have to deal much with this floor —we have a private cleaning company come vacuum whenever it's needed."

Nora leaned forward, "Excuse me? I thought I might be hired on as a cook here, that's what I did at my last job."

"So sorry I didn't mention it over the phone, but I thought I might be able to talk you into it in person. The available position we have is in housekeeping, but I think over time we could try and move you into the kitchen when a spot opens, that is unless you come to like the position."

Nora ran a hand through her hair and licked her lips to speak.

"Before you say anything," said Tressa, "It's higher pay, and you'll still have access to the pool once a week like the other employees."

A single thought pierced Nora's mind—pulling back into her old job's parking lot and walking into that dull two-story building.

Nora said, "You know, I guess I could give it a shot."

"So great to hear, I knew I could persuade you. Now, let me ask a few more questions before I get you a key card and pair you up with your trainer for the day."

"You want me to start today?"

"Well on the phone you said you have all day free, I thought it would be best to throw you right into the deep end, as they say."

Nora thought of Bart, who had already planned a marathon of Universal's horror classics later on, but Tressa's eyes pressed on her, unblinking.

Nora took a breath in, smiled, and said, "I suppose that would be fine with me."

"Great," said Tressa, "let's continue."

2:05 PM SATURDAY

Nora stood outside the elevator doors of the 11th floor, gazing across a cafeteria nearly as big as the parking lot. Soft white lights lit row after row of mostly empty tables. Hallways extended out in the four cardinal directions from the main hall—the cafeteria as it so happened to be on this floor.

Tressa had explained that each floor above hers served a function, though many were entirely housing. A pool for water aerobics on one floor, a low impact gym on another. One of them was apparently filled with cots for employees to sleep on a long shift.

The golden elevator doors opened behind her, and a voice said, "So, you're the new recruit around here huh?" The woman stepped around Nora and continued, "Looks like they gave you the uniform already, so I won't have to show you where those are. If you need extra shirts they dock it from your pay, so don't lose what you got. Boss said I'd be training you this evening in the fine art of cleaning the old folk's rooms."

"I'm Nora. you got it on the uniform, I won't misplace this *stellar* shirt. This graphic looks like it's from the 80's."

The woman looked unamused, "Name's Ellie. Were you even alive back then?"

Nora said, "Not quite, but I like pretty much every movie they made back then more than the one's they make these days. Practical effects all the way."

Ellie said, "So you're a fan of *The Thing*?"

"John Carpenter can do no wrong as far as I'm concerned."

"Ditto. Anyway, we should get going if I'm going to show you everything before I leave—Not sure if Tressa mentioned I'll be leaving at five and need you to cover my night shift."

Nora asked, "You want me to cover your night shift on my first day?"

"Look, I don't *want* you to, I need you too. I'll get you back, don't worry."

"I had this whole monster marathon thing scheduled with a friend—"

Ellie's eyes went wide as she said, "Please please please? I'll give you all my horror movies to barrow."

"Fine, what the hell," Nora threw a hand in the air, "I can cover it. But you better have some niche movies in your collection, I like hidden gems—don't bother bringing Freddy or Jason type stuff, I have all that in Hi-Def. Now teach me everything quick because I don't want to be running around here at three in the morning like a chicken with my head cut off."

Ellie said, "You got it you got it, we just have to go grab a pair of cleaning carts to wheel around. Have you seen *Mad God*?"

Nora said, "Love it! I'll watch anything filmed with stop motion; it makes every movement look so creepy. I can't get enough."

"In that case I'll give you the deluxe tour."

4:45 PM SATURDAY

Nora and Ellie stood on the blue and white mosaic tiling inside the water aerobics studio of the seventh floor.

Ellie said, "Okay that almost does it for what I can teach you on your first day. Now this last thing is important," She clapped her hands, "Covering the pool at night! roughly 9 PM. You would think locking the door would be enough, but when this place first opened one of the oldies somehow busted in and took a dive after hours. They never came back up for air."

Nora looked over the pool with uneasy fascination, "Really? That happened here?"

"Happened, sad to say. Although I hear most others who stay here pass peacefully, it's a state-of-the-art kind of place. Just remember to unspool this covering over the water and connect the hooks at the end to the hooks at the corner of the pool. Besides that, we don't have to deal with the chemicals for it or anything, a private company does that. We can spot check the water with those nets over there." Ellie pointed across the pool where a few elderly residents of the Super Elite kicked from end to end, "Oh and one more thing, don't goof off when the night nurse is around, she's got the eyes of a raven, I swear. Any questions?"

"Nevermore." Said Nora, and both laughed.

"In that case I'm going to drop off my cart in the cafeteria closet then head to the breakroom to grab my things and get out of here. Want to ride up with me?"

Nora said, "sounds like a plan, I'll talk to the cook about getting something to eat, I need fuel for the night shift."

Ellie turned to the door and said, "You got it, Nor. Thanks again for covering me. I hope you stick around."

Nora pushed her cart behind Ellie through the open frosted glass door and heard the locking mechanism click shut. Down the hall, the middle of the three employee elevators opened and they stepped inside.

"How's the food around here?" Asked Nora, standing beside Ellie while the golden doors closed.

Ellie said, "I guess you'll find out soon enough." She pressed the button marked '11' for the cafeteria. Lower on the panel, Nora noticed that the fourteenth floor, the level below Tressa's office, had a key icon beside it.

Nora asked, "is that floor for us?"

Ellie pointed to the small black card reader beside the button panel, "You'd need a different key card, I don't really know any of the employees who have them. Probably business types, you know."

The elevator opened on the cafeteria. Nora stepped out after Ellie, staying to look at the button a moment longer, only noticing the jaunty music humming from inside once she stepped out. Residents were congregating in the cafeteria having dinner, having a chat. They smiled and Nora smiled back as she pushed her cart to the corner near an empty table.

After getting through half a plate of vegetable lasagna, Nora left the table to toss her food in the garbage. It tasted fine, but for some reason the spinach layered between the pasta reminded her of a movie she hadn't seen since childhood.

She whispered, "Soylent Green is people!" as she scrapped her remaining food into the trash.

8:30 PM SATURDAY

The final rays of sunset glowed through the curtains of a newly vacant resident's room while Nora cleaned it. She pulled one of the curtains back revealing a window looking onto the outside world. Even though Ellie already explained it, the depth of field in the screen projecting the image was impressive. Nora imagined a window looking out onto what was really there, a wall of dense earth, like being buried alive.

She let go of the curtains and turned, looking over the work she had done. Except for a single piece of paper poking out from under the dresser, the room was tidy and ready for someone new. She picked up the paper and read the first line printed on it, '*Obscura Initiative Protocol*', before crumpling it up and throwing it in the trash.

Pushing the cleaning cart out of the room, Nora thought aloud, "Onto the next one." And another, darker, thought, "What's the turnover rate in this place?"

The hallway of floor five, a level consisting of resident apartments and a few nurse stations, stretched out before her.

Someone behind her said, "What did you say?"

Nora's lungs tightened and a shiver ran up her spine. "Sorry," she turned, "I didn't see you there."

A woman wearing scrubs stood with her back arrow straight and a pen tucked behind her ear. She held a clipboard under her arm so tight it looked like it might snap in half.

"I'm sure you didn't," the nurses nose pinched, "This must be day one for you."

Nora did not break eye contact. "Matter of fact it is, and my trainer left a while ago. Can I do anything to help?"

"I can handle my job on my own, I hope you can do the same."

Nora was heating up, burning with a venomous vocabulary that needed to escape her lips. She took a deep breath and remembered as many Twilight Zone episodes as she could to clear her mind.

Nora said, "Rod Serling, you were a genius."

The nurse said, "What on earth are you talking about? if you really need someone to make an itemized list for you, start by lending your skills to Apartment 517 near the end of the hall, that resident will not be returning."

"Now that you mention it, I can't waste any more time speaking with you." Nora smiled with all the scorn she could manage then turned back to her cart and went down the hallway without looking back, continuing the list of Twilight Zone episodes in her mind until she felt the crone of a nurse vanish into an empty apartment behind her.

Further down the hall Nora realized what she thought was a dead-end was an intersection that split left and right; a sign on the wall pointed her left toward 550-500. The amber tone of wall mounted sconces glowed faintly and a mirror at the far end of the section made the passage look almost infinite. Nora's reflection looked back at her from the mirror, watching her every move.

"Do they really need to turn the lights so low at night?" she pushed her cart down the hallway listening to a rapidly worsening rattle from the front right wheel. The section started at

550, but as Nora approached the mirror, the rooms were still in the 540's.

"How do any of the residents find their way around this place?" Nora came to another fork in the road, a split with a sign by the mirror pointing right for rooms 520-500. The lights were dimmed further in the adjacent hallways and when Nora came to room 517 She could only count a few lights that were left on at all.

Nora thought aloud, "If they're trying to save money on energy they better think of a different solution, I'm not working in the dark every time I'm scheduled for a night shift."

She took her Super Elite employee key card from her pocket and swiped it through the lock. A green light by the door flashed and the lock shifted open. Inside, the lights worked fine and Nora got to work cleaning, surprised at how disheveled the place was.

"For someone who must have been on the verge of passing, you sure knew how to throw a rager, huh?"

After an hour she pushed her cart back into the hallway, eager to return to the elevator lobby where she knew all the lights would be on.

"I thought you were braver than this," she said to herself, "A dark hallway has you scared now?"

But the hallway seemed different. Now, not a single amber light was on. To her left the passage extended into shadows. To her right, an exit sign glowed red at the end of the hall.

"Hello?" Nora felt the word escape before she could pull it back. "I guess I am that scared," she said with a forced laugh as the door to room 517 closed behind her. "I'd even take help from that uptight nurse right now. Where the hell did she skitter off to?"

The hairs on the back of her neck rose as the lock to room 517 clicked shut. The front wheel of her cart whined it's steady warning as Nora made her way toward the crimson light of the exit.

11 PM SATURDAY

The sign did not say exit, at least not in any language she knew of. Nora held her hand on the cold metal door beneath the sign, deciding if she should walk back the way she came. Gazing back into the darkness again, she pressed into the door and pulled her cart behind, walking into the blinding light.

As the door locked behind her, Nora's vision returned, and she found herself standing back at the fifth-floor elevator lobby. The golden doors on the leftmost employee elevator opened without prompt.

Nora stared at the open elevator.

She thought aloud, "I'm getting all turned around in the place. and I know I'm missing something."

The elevator doors began closing in front of her. "I forgot about the pools!" she exclaimed and reached out, stopping the door before it could close. She stepped inside, more worried about a resident drowning because of her forgetfulness than of the halls around room 517.

The hallways on the water aerobics floor were sparsely lit with the same amber sconces as the fifth floor, but Nora kept moving. With a swipe of her card, she unlocked the frosted glass door to the pool. The smell of chlorine felt like a permeable wall as she stepped through it. Nora felt a wash of relief pass over her as she looked around the room—another staff member had already covered the pool.

She said, "Thank the gods," and shrugged off the stress.

Something pressed against the underside of the pool cover and all the relief Nora felt was gone.

"What the hell!" Nora shouted and ran to the side of the pool, crouching along the edge. She waited for movement, anything that would confirm what she saw.

"My eyes can't be playing tricks." she said, still watching the pool cover intently, "That was too real."

She got the feeling she should not be standing so close to the water. Nora took a few steps back without taking her eyes from the pool cover, but slipped on the wet tile, falling to the mosaic floor.

"Fuck!" she cried out, rubbing a point of throbbing pain on the side of her head as she stared up at the blurry ceiling.

The sound of water splashing under the pool cover interrupted her daze and she turned to see something inhuman pressing up through the center. Her heart jumped in her chest and fear overtook every function in her body. Standing best she could, Nora ran out the door toward the elevator lobby without looking back.

Nora rubbed the side of her head trying to make sense of everything, "I'm getting the hell out of this place; I didn't sign up for this." She tapped at the elevator call button over and over, focusing on the seam of the golden doors that would open and take her back to a world she could understand.

standing inside and the doors closed behind her, the swinging 1920s elevator music struck a certain chord in Nora. She considered going back to the pool, that she should do everything in her power to help the person who was probably drowning; that anyone in their right mind would go back—would have never left.

But the image of an inhuman shape pressing out of the pool

63

flashed on the back of her eyelids with every blink, burning in her mind. She pressed the button inside the elevator for the parking garage while trying her best not to close her eyes. Instead, she focused on the crystals hanging from the miniature chandelier.

When she noticed the elevator wasn't moving, she tried the garage button again, and again. Then she pressed for the cafeteria, then every other floor from one to thirteen. Nora ran her hand across the panel, pressing each button from top to bottom. Without trying, she pressed the button for floor 14.

A red light blinked on the small key card reader beside the panel. Nora pulled her card from her pocket, knowing from what Ellie told her that it was hopeless to try. She swiped her card anyway and watched the red light blink green.

The elevator began its descent.

12 AM SUNDAY

The music inside the elevator car was no longer calming—nothing about the Super Elite was calming. To Nora, it felt more like a crypt then a retirement home, and she was only going deeper. The lights of the miniature chandelier flickered as the golden doors of the elevator slid open on floor 14.

A well-lit hallway stretched out before her with no visible windows or pictures on the wall. A few black-glass domes on the ceiling made Nora think she was being watched.

"Is anyone down here?" She said, walking slowly out of the elevator. The doors closed behind her, and she listened to the sound of the elevator being pulled back toward the surface, taking the faint old timey music along with it.

Nobody answered, but she could hear the whirring sound of machines somewhere close.

"I'm coming down the hallway, if there is anyone here that cares. And... and I'm incredibly violent!" Nora laughed nervously, trying to recognize and quell the great fear beating through her heart.

Moving forward, the sound of radio fuzz caught her attention. With a deep breath and teeth clenched she rushed onward, too afraid to prolong her fears by walking slow

Nora came to a turn at the end of hall and ran into an unmarked door, pushing through it and falling to the floor. A bruise was forming on the side of her head where she fell in the water aerobics room, now the pain doubled.

She looked up from the unmarked floor and fought to hold back a scream. The room was cramped with strange machines covering the walls and a large tubular tank filled with liquid— and a human.

"It can't be…" She was momentarily lost trying to comprehend what she was seeing. Suspended in yellow liquid, the body of a man was connected to countless wires and tubes that looked disturbingly organic. His hair was gone and his eyes were pressed tightly closed.

Nora blinked, focusing and refocusing. "What in all hells is this place?"

Screens along one wall displayed documents and diagrams Nora didn't understand. All except for one phrase she saw somewhere earlier, *Obscura Initiative Protocol.*

Nora looked around the room, glancing back to the man every few seconds, unable to look away. "Where have I seen those words before? What does it mean?"

A desk next to the glass tank had a clipboard and the noisy radio on it. Nora slammed her fist down on the radio, but instead of falling apart, the station changed and the whirring machines in the room were masked by the voice of a radio host.

"—and thanks for listening with me, Barry Valentine on FM 99.9, as I take you through the long haul tonight. In a little under an hour, you'll be taken bake to another era in music with your nightly dose of Twilight Time, but for now let's keep rockin' to the classics." The track turned over and CCR's 'It Came Out of the Sky' crackled through the radio's speaker.

Bubbles rose in the liquid of the tank as the man inside swayed slowly back and forth. Nora stepped to the glass and said, "Hey you! Are you alive in there?"

The man's eyes strained open, bloodshot and dilated. Nora

jumped back a few steps but kept eye contact—she saw pain, nothing else.

She said, "I'm going to get you out of this, well, whatever this thing is." and went to the desk where the clipboard rested. She grabbed it and read the scribbled notes. The name Garfield Anderson was scratched on the top, with a list of physical and mental characteristics below.

"You're Garfield?" She said, staring into the glass.

Bubbled lifted around his face as he stared from inside the glass tank.

She flipped a piece of paper over on the clipboard.

Nora read aloud, "Obscura Drive?" Look, I don't know what any of this means but I'm getting you out of here whether I know how or not."

Setting the clipboard down she looked around the tank for a release mechanism and found a small latch affixed to the back near the ceiling. Nora moved a chair out from under the desk and stood on it while reaching for the latch. She slid the latch aside revealing a pale green button and pressed it. The whirring of the machines around her slowed and she heard liquid passing through a drain.

Nora stepped off the chair and watched the amber liquid inside the glass tank drain through the bottom while Garfield stretched his arms and legs inside the tank, tearing free from the tubes and wires connected to him. He stood shaking as the liquid drained and the glass around him lowered a space beneath the floor.

Nora stared, "Garfield?" She extended a hand slowly.

He recoiled and said, "Are you here to run more tests on me?"

"Tests? Listen I don't even know what this place is. I just saw a human in a tank and couldn't let you stay in that thing. My name is Nora. What is this place? What are they do to you?"

Garfield cleared his throat and said, "Nora, you must escape before it's too late."

She looked around, "The elevator won't take me back up."

Garfield straightened his posture best he could, pulling loose a few more wires as he did. He exhaled slow and said, "I know another way. You'll have to come with me."

"Can you walk? Or run? We need to get the hell out of here."

Garfield turned and Nora gasped. His back was covered in writhing tentacles almost thick as fur, many of the tubes she thought came from the glass tank were appendages sprouting from his body. Garfield paid no mind and pressed a series of buttons beside a large panel on the wall. The panel slid back, revealing another, larger room.

"This way," he looked back and nodded to her, "They have something I can use to help you. But you must brace yourself."

"For what? What about you?"

"It is too late for me," Garfield glanced toward his back, then gestured to the entirety of the room, "It is too late for us."

Nora gazed across the newly opened room. She saw rows and rows of glass tanks identical to the one Garfield had been suspended in. Each contained a body, each body twisted into a different, striking form.

"No," said Nora, "What are you showing me? This can't be real."

Garfield limped to a podium in front of the glass tanks where a small metallic object rested. Nora heard radio static coming from it.

"This is real, Nora. This is a madman's workshop. A place far beyond the void. And It's all because of this."

Garfield picked up the metal object and handed it to the tentacles on his back. Each one gripped at it, pulling it to the center of his spine.

He continued, "The Obscura Drive. A wormhole generator. In all their work to understand it, I've been the only success."

"What do you mean?"

"I know how to use it." Garfield coughed, "I was the one who found it, in another lifetime."

"What about you? I can't leave you and all of these people."

Garfield said, "It's not so simple. This the only way I can help you." and coughed up a handful of blood. Nora stared at him for a moment, trying to understand. Suddenly a blaring alarm filled the room.

"This is the only way." Garfield repeated, his bloodshot eyes shaking.

The sound of security personnel clattered toward them from somewhere close as the alarm continued. Nora stood frozen in her tracks. The glass tanks were real, the mutations were real, and it would happen to her unless Garfield could set her free.

"Okay." She said, "I'm ready."

Garfield replied, "Thank you for releasing me, Nora. It was nice to breath air again, even just for a little while."

Light shined from the metallic object at Garfield's back as his many tentacles reached outward like the rays of the sun. He stood there like a many-armed god, staring at Nora with a look of hope through crimson scorched eyes. The light grew brighter until Garfield was encircled by it, and still the sounds of people rushing toward them grew louder.

Nora took a deep breath and reached out to Garfield as his arm extended toward her.

"Good luck out there, Nora."

A bolt of blue lightning flashed between them. A cloud of glimmering dust filled the room. The pungent smell of ozone hung in the air.

As the silvery dust settled around Garfield, half a dozen guards circled him. He studied the room. Nora escaped.

But something felt wrong to Garfield. With greater and greater fear, he wondered, where in all the vast cosmos he might have sent her.

Made in the USA
Columbia, SC
24 November 2024

47024855R00045